I

to say YES!

Other titles in the bunch:

Baby Bear Comes Home
Big Dog and Little Dog Visit the Moon
Delilah Digs for Treasure Dilly and the Goody-Goody
Horse in the House I Don't Want to Say Yes!
Juggling with Jeremy Keeping Secrets
Mabel and Max Magnificent Mummies
Midnight at Memphis Mouse Flute
The Nut Map Owl in the House
Riff-Raff Rabbit Rosie and the Robbers
Runaway Fred Tom's Hats

First published in Great Britain 1998
By Egmont Books Ltd,
239 Kensington High St, London W8 6SA
Published in hardback by Heinemann Library,
a division of Reed Educational and Professional Publishing Ltd
by arrangement with Egmont Books Ltd.
Text copyright © Bel Mooney 1998
Illustrations copyright © Margaret Chamberlain 1998
The author and illustrator have asserted their moral rights
Paperback ISBN 1 4052 0138 X
Hardback ISBN 0 4349 7655 5
10 9 8 7 6
A CIP catalogue record for this title is available from the British Library.
Printed and bound in the U.A.E.

Bel Mooney

I don't want to say YES!

Illustrated by Margaret Chamberlain

BLue Bananas

Kitty had one favourite word.

It was No. She answered, 'No!'

to everything.

Would you like some new shoes?

No!

When Mum asked her if she wanted

to go to the park, she said, 'No!'

Do you want to play on the swings?

No!

When her brother,
Dan, asked her if she
wanted to play with
him, she said, 'No!'

Shall I build you a house?

No!

7

When Dad asked her to sit on his knee and read a book, she said, 'No!'

Shall we read your new book?

It wasn't that Kitty didn't like going to the park, or playing with Dan, or reading with Dad. It was just that she didn't like saying, 'Yes'.

No!

One day, Kitty and Dan were in the garden. They were playing with Copper, the cat from next door. It began to rain.

I'll collect Copper later.

Mum called from the kitchen window, 'Come inside, you two, or you'll get soaked.'

Quickly!

OK, Mum!

No!

Dan went in, but Kitty just went on riding her bike round and round in the rain.

She rode through the puddles.

She shook the rain off her hair.

She brushed

the drops off

her sweater.

15

She stamped in the puddles.

Then she ran

around stamping

everywhere.

STAMP
STAMP
STAMP

Kitty liked being in the garden. There was no one out there to tell her what to do.

I don't want to go in!

17

But soon Kitty was soaking.
She grew tired of playing in
the rain. She didn't like the
swishing noise of the trees.

Brrr

She was bored and she was beginning to feel cold. So was Copper.

I'm fed up!

Me too.

19

Slowly, Kitty and Copper walked closer to the house.

20

Then, very slowly, they went inside.

Soon be dry, Copper.

21

Oh, Kitty!

As they crept across the kitchen, they left puddles on the floor. Mum sighed.

22

'Look at you, you're soaking wet,' Mum said. 'You'll catch cold unless we change your clothes.'

'Won't!' said Kitty.

Come back here, Kitty!

'Kitty! Come here at once and change those wet clothes!'

'No, no, no!' said Kitty as she ran up the stairs.

In the bedroom, Mum pushed

and pulled Kitty into dry clothes.

26

'You can stay in your room until tea,' Mum said crossly. 'See if you can learn to say, "Yes!" for a change.'

You can come out now, Copper.

When Mum had gone, Kitty asked her
bears if they liked her. But they
didn't say, 'Yes'.

Nobody likes me.

Kitty made

a castle with

her bricks.

She asked the

bricks if they

liked her

- but they all

fell

down.

Kitty asked her books how to say, 'Yes'.

There were lots of words inside them,

but they were silent.

The only word that came from

Kitty's mouth was a very angry, 'No!'

NO!

It was teatime and
Mum called Kitty
for tea. Kitty was hungry.
She walked slowly,

step

by step,

down

the stairs.

Kitty sat in her

chair and ate her tea,

but she didn't say anything.

Dan teased her. 'What's the matter, Kitty? Lost your tongue?'

Kitty glared at him. Then she kicked at him under the table and shouted.

She was cross with everyone and

everyone was cross with her.

35

After tea, Kitty lined up her toys and told them how bad they were.

Come in here now! Take off those wet clothes.

36

Dad sat in the armchair reading his newspaper. Now and then he looked up at Kitty and smiled.

'It's time for bed, Kitty,' Mum called.

'Go and kiss Dad goodnight.'

Kitty didn't want to.

Hurry up Kitty!

39

Dad pretended to read his newspaper. He knew Kitty very well. He pretended he didn't want a kiss.

I don't want you to kiss me.

'Whatever you do, don't kiss me,' he said. 'You mustn't be a good girl, and most of all you mustn't say, "Yes!" or I will turn into a terrible monster.'

'Now, remember, you don't want to kiss me goodnight, do you?'

Kitty smiled for the first time that day.

And what do you think she said?

43

Dad started to chase Kitty.

I'm coming to get you!

45

Dad caught Kitty and gave her a big

hug. Mum and Dan laughed.

'Would you like me to read you a story,

Shall we read your new book?

now?' asked Dad.

And this time Kitty knew exactly what to say . . .

Yes!

48